For
The lady who always lends an ear to my ceaseless chatter
and who holds my hand as we journey through life, the lady I
call Mom. and Eleonore Hope –The stars in your eyes are my
raison d'être.

Mommy Says
Veronica Lin
Illustrated by Katerina Khlebnikova
Published by Ching Cheng Construction
25F-5, No. 402, Zhengshi Road, Xitun District, Taichung City 407
04-2254-9333
First Printing, 2024
ISBN 978-626-98742-0-0

Mommy Says

Veronica Lin

Illustrated by
Katerina Khlebnikova

The morning sunlight sneaks through the gaps in the curtains, warming the crisp autumn air. Before my eyes even open, I hear the pitter-patter of lively footsteps approaching, accompanied by the enchanting voice of a soprano....

While I flip pancakes, you dance to the rhythm of the sizzling skillet. One song after another, we sing your favorite tunes together. You invent funny lyrics and melodies that are uniquely ours. You know what, dear child? Your laughter is my favorite music.

You have a very special sense of fashion.

Radiating endless energy, you tug my arm
eagerly to set out and conquer the world.

Mommy says, when seeing people, say hello!
Hello, doggy! Hello, puffy clouds! Hello, beautiful day!

We share a buttery croissant, as we cross a bridge filled with love locks.
Sometimes, you joyfully skip along the Seine, while other times you pause
to peek into shop windows. Like a little bird that keeps asking "why?",
you chirp away about your discoveries and wonders along the way.

Hand in hand, we stroll along winding cobblestone streets, wander through bustling markets, saunter by the Palais Garnier, visit a charming florist full of vibrant blooms, caper across squares with statues of serious men on horseback, and toss a coin to make a wish in a gleaming fountain.

Mommy says, before crossing the road,
look left, look right, ready..... and..... go!

Finally, we arrive at Monceau Park.

Mommy says, Shhhhh!
dinosaurs might be napping under the slides.

Amidst the melodies of birdsong, branches gently sway in the breeze. Everything is golden and bronze, with a delicate touch of ochre, amber and green. We play a game of stepping stones on fallen leaves and collect pine cones as we search for dinosaur footprints. Towering rocks serve as our fortress, as you, a valiant knight, ride gallantly on the carousel.

Mommy says, playing together is more fun.

Mommy says, we can create anything we want, like
an airplane that takes us around the world,
a castle tall enough to embrace the moon, or
even a beautiful lavender field.

I build your dreams, and you fulfill mine.

I let go of your tiny hand and watch you chase after
the squirrels. Your bouncy little steps are like
the fluttering wings of a butterfly, brimming with
excitement, almost ready to take flight. My heart
dances with each of your cheerful hops,
as we soar together in a world of wonder.

Mommy says, going a bit slower is how we make friends with the squirrels.

We savor delicious crêpes and hot chocolate at a café, where the sound of chatter and clinking teaspoons blend harmoniously with the jazz. A lazy cat naps at our feet. Sunlight filters through the leaves, casting a dappled glow on your beaming face. In the next moment, "splish-splash"!, an impromptu rain could catch us unawares, leaving us soaking wet. Your infectious laughter echoes as we jump and splash in puddles. Happiness, as it turns out, is so simple.

Mommy says, there is always a rainbow after the rain.

Mommy says, don't be afraid!

Mommy is always here.
Always.

As twilight turns into night, the delightful scent of roses fills the air in Tuileries Garden.

When you look up at me, with a smile that lights up the evening sky, and sweetly say, "Mommy...," I see my reflection in your bright eyes. And you, my precious one, are the most profound imprint on my journey. Together, we traverse the city bathed in golden hues, hand in hand.

Mommy says, the sun is asleep, whales are asleep,
cats are asleep, even ladybugs hide between petals,
closing their wings.

We lose ourselves in tales of adventures in faraway lands, carried away by the wings of imagination. After countless lullabies and once-upon-a-times, your eyelids grow heavy with the weight of slumber, while a gentle smile lingers on your lips. I gaze at your peacefully sleeping face, hoping it could slow down time. Holding you close, our hearts beat as one.

Mommy says, there are more stars in the universe than there are snowflakes in a snow globe—like, a gazillion trillion! And each star has its very own story to tell.

In the infinite night sky, you shine with a unique brilliance.
Now, you stand at the beginning of an adventure,
where the path may be rocky, with valleys and hills to navigate.
May your heart always sparkle with curiosity.
May your laughter be unrestrained, your spirit untamed.
May you find joy in every blooming flower and every tender breeze that
caresses your face.
May you forever be inspired by the beauty of life and discover strength
within the depths of your heart.

Mommy says, no matter what happens, I will always love you. Mommy says, thank you for making me the happiest person in the world. My sunshine, my moonlight, my Valentine.

Origin of Creation

This story draws inspiration from a day in the life of my daughter and me. As my daughter takes her first steps into language, she imitates my words like a little parrot, punctuating her sentences with "Mommy says…. Mommy says….", and blends them with her own invented language—a funny mixture that fills our home with laughter and surprises. Through her innocent eyes, I am reminded of the simple pleasures that often elude our attention amidst the hustle and bustle of daily life. Throughout our day, we create memories filled with simple joy and shared laughter— from the delightful breakfast concert to a leisurely stroll through our beloved spots, then to adventures into nature, and culminating in gleeful play in the rain. Finally, the day gently winds down with our bedtime routine, as we dive into imaginative worlds before sharing a serene moment of tender embrace. Regardless of the weather or what we do, our greatest joy is simply being together. This seemingly ordinary day is, for us, truly unique.

This is also a story about the timeless bond between a mother and her children across generations. In the gaze of my daughter, I'm transported back to the moment when I, too, looked up and called out to my own mother with boundless love and admiration. In that fleeting moment of connection, I find contentment, strength, and an overwhelming sense of fulfillment.

Just as our parents have stood by us, our commitment to our children remains unwavering. Time spent with children cannot be rewound. Cradle them a bit longer, revel in their radiant smiles, for they stay little for such a short while. I am profoundly grateful for every shared moment and for the deep connection every "Mommy" brings. I hope you can find resonance with our day and harvest abundant laughter and joy along the extraordinary journey of parenthood!

About the Author

The author graduated from Boston University and ESSEC Business School, with majors in Business Administration and French Literature. Following her passion, she furthered her studies in art history at Ecole du Louvre in Paris. A girl who once sought after beautiful things and galloped freely through forests on horseback later blossomed into a loving mother of two. This transition sparked a profound interest in children's literature, leading to the successful completion of a certificate in Child Psychology from the University of Geneva. For the author, the greatest happiness lies in sharing her creations with children. She is also the author of *Little Seashell*.

About the Illustrator

Raised in a family of book lovers, Katerina Khlebnikova dreamt of being an artist from a very young age. A graduate of the Moscow State University Ivan Fedorov, Faculty of Graphic Arts, she is a member of the Moscow Union of Artists (Department of Prints). She has participated in numerous exhibitions, both in Russia and elsewhere, and is a winner at Moscow's International Festival of Book Illustration and Visual Literature (MORS). She has created artwork for books published in Russia, China, Serbia, Spain and Canada. Katerina has two children.